BOOM! BANG! BOOM

Mara taps on pots and pans.

"Not now, Mara," says Abba.
"It's time to cook Shabbat dinner."

Not Now, Mara!

Enjoy!
AvivaB.

story by Aviva L. Brown

To my Love, my Miriam, my sweet, precocious girl
--A.B.

BONUS CONTENT HERE: www.avivabrown.com/marabonus

Names: Brown, Aviva L., author. | Aveeta, Mia, illustrator.
Title: Not now, Mara! / Aviva L. Brown ; Mia Aveeta, illustrator.
Description: Greensboro, NC : SpringLight Publishing, 2020. | Summary: As her parents prepare for Shabbat, a precocious toddler tries to play her favorite games only to be told, "Not now, Mara!"
Identifiers: LCCN 2020914541 (print) | ISBN 978-1-7335967-3-2 (hardcover) | ISBN 978-1-7335967-4-9 (softcover)
Subjects: LCSH: Picture books for children. | High interest-low vocabulary books. | CYAC: Judaism--Fiction. | Sabbath--Fiction. | Toddlers--Fiction. | Family life--Fiction. | Racially mixed people--Fiction. | BISAC: JUVENILE FICTION / Religious / Jewish. | JUVENILE FICTION / Diversity & Multicultural.
Classification: LCC PZ7.1.B792 No 2020 (print) | LCC PZ7.1.B792 (ebook) | DDC [E]--dc23.

Mara toddles into the dining room.

Puppy dances under the table.
Mara crawls after her.

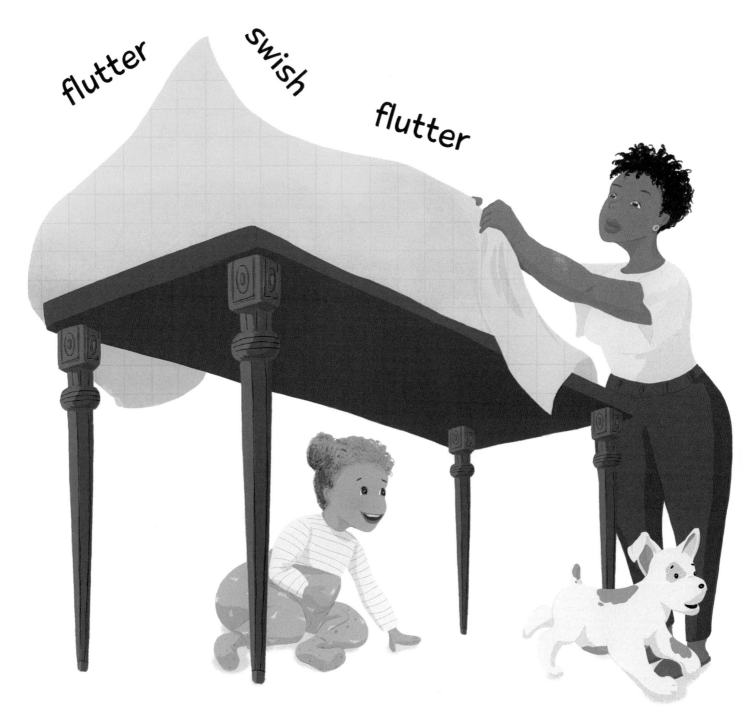

A tablecloth falls softly all around.

Mara bumps Mommy's foot.

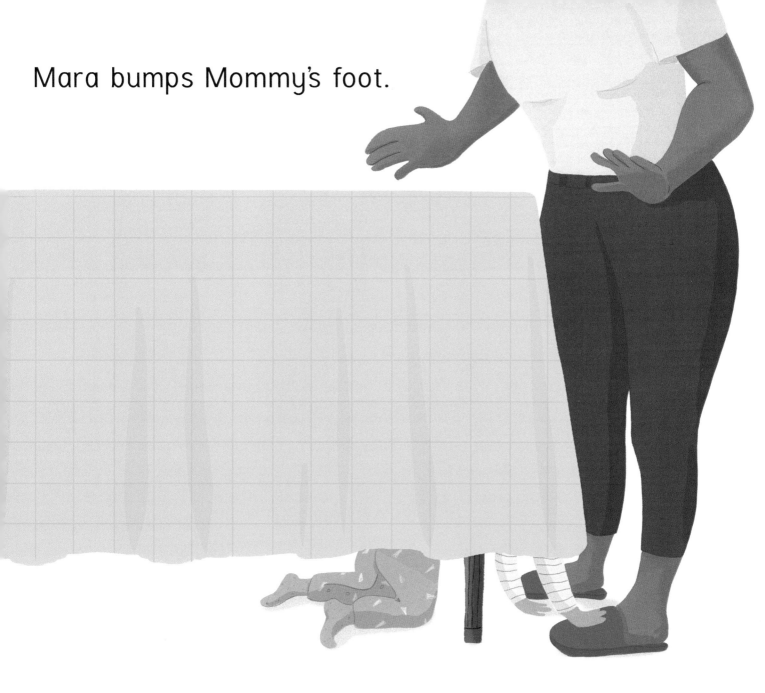

"**OUCH!** Not under the table, Mara. Not now."

Mara sees pretty flowers,
just like outside.

Onto the chair goes Mara.

Mara picks petals one by one.

"Not now, Mara," Abba says.
"We don't pluck these flowers!"

TEETER!
TOTTER!
TEETER!

Mara peeks through the window

"It's not time now," says Mommy.
"Soon."

Mara waits.

She sees
Bubbe and Zayde.

Inside, Zayde scoops Mara into a hug.

"Hello, shayna punim," says Bubbe.
She kisses Mara's cheek.

Mara grabs at two loaves of braided
challah in Bubbe's basket.
"Not now, Mara," Bubbe says, laughing.

Mommy lights two candles.

She sings a blessing.
Everyone says, "Shabbat Shalom!"

Abba, Mommy, Bubbe, and Zayde announce,

"Now, Mara!"

Mara smiles.
"Sabbat Salom!"

Made in the USA
Columbia, SC
10 September 2020